The Murders at Hobson's

Coal Hole and

The Prospect of Whitby

ILLUSTRATIONS; Acknowledgements

Our new cover, designed by Elizabeth Mills, shows a striking study of Sherlock Holmes made by Sidney Paget, the most prolific of the artists in the canon. Paget made this definitive image only four years before his death in 1908.

The Annotated Sherlock Holmes [two massive volumes edited by William S. Baring-Gould, published by John Murray, 1968] notes the use for advertising of the popular [vulgar?] concept of Holmes's appearance, *circa* 1900, with a rendering in aid of "Grand Cut" pipe tobacco, probably from the collection of Judge Kenneth G. Brill [1883-1954] of St Paul, Minnesota. The caption read:

Holmes: "Now *there*'s a tobacco you could smoke all day without burning your tongue."

Watson: "*Amazing, Holmes!*"

Holmes: "Elementary, My dear Watson --It's **Grand Cut**-- Never burns the tongue of old or young."

We have retained this illustration as a frontispiece because it shows [particularly at Dr Watson's expense] how the popularity of Holmes was rapidly and crassly exploited for commercial purposes in the United States.

There is an image at the back of the book, drawn from the Wikimedia Commons, of The Prospect of Whitby as it is today, substantially unchanged from the tavern as it appeared in Watson's day. It is owned by a large brewing corporation but has become a place of pilgrimage, claiming to be the British public house most often visited by visitors from abroad.

~0~

DEDICATION

To my friend and other friends of Henry Smith, M.P., this book is dedicated: with wishes for a merry May, 2015

The Murders at Hobson's Coal Hole and

The Prospect of Whitby

(Further Cases of Sherlock Holmes by Oliver St. Gaudy)

Copyright by Oliver St. Gaudy, 2015

ISBN: 978-1507732885

~o~0~o~

Further Cases of Sherlock Holmes

Related by Doctor John H. Watson

The only known manuscripts of the stories in this collection are rough bundles of modern papers without provenance, in the collection of Oliver St Gaudy, by whom they have been revised and otherwise prepared for publication. The pages are in various hands, and contain several interpolations made by one hand, in badly faded green ink, apparently for the sake of inserting connective material, perhaps in an early attempt at editing. It is not claimed that any parts of these manuscripts are the work of Sir Arthur Conan Doyle. Moreover, the texts as now given differ in internal order and structure, and no claim is made that all are simply as supposedly written by Doctor Watson with the hot breath of Holmes on the back of his neck. The aim here is merely to provide some further interest for the reader of *credible* extensions of the canon: Watson is seen showing some change in style after Holmes has gone. The reader will be the judge of any pleasure or the opposite. Here also are no fantastic tin trunk discoveries at garage sales. And there are no fairy stories. The Watson diaries, of course, are yet to be found.

Oliver St Gaudy
Three Bridges, West Sussex, 2015

The Murders at Hobson's Coal Hole and The Prospect of Whitby

Readers will be glad to hear that my friend Mr Sherlock Holmes made a rapid recovery from the self-inflicted causes of the 'deadly disease' with which he trapped an ingenious poisoner, not long after our return from a coastal marshland venture in the unhappy case of a lost champion of free speech, probably never to be completely resolved. Unhappy for me also, content to live a quiet domestic life as a private physician when not actually playing my part as the occasional assistant of the great consulting detective.

For my pains, I was left facing the prospect of being the single so-styled 'independent' witness at the Old Bailey in what promised to be a sensational trial. Other medical men would regard this situation, fairly or not, as disgraceful to our profession. Near certainty that the villain would be hanged [if not detained at Her Majesty's pleasure as a lunatic] would not lessen my chances of being feathered by my fellow practitioners after being tarred by appearing in so disgraceful a context: I was the only person other than Holmes who had heard the poisoner confess to one murder, and admit attempting another --to destroy Holmes. This knowledge made certain that I would face the onslaught of defending counsel

1

anxious to cast doubt on my respectability and integrity as a witness, because of the known relationship between me and the world's most famous consulting detective. Holmes's evidence would be seriously impeached on the ground that he and the accused were personal enemies. And all this, let it be marked, without the inevitable notoriety also consequent on my having obligingly skulked behind the sickbed of a 'patient' --which was how my truly unheroic actions in 'The Adventure of the Dying Detective' would be represented in our most disreputable public prints.

I had never joined Holmes to work on two investigations simultaneously; he may have done so, but to my knowledge he was true to his principle of applying his undivided powers to any challenge he deemed worthy of his steel. Then, however, there came to him by the post one morning a pretty little ivory box made to inflict a poisonous stab when opened. This he recognized as a mortal challenge from a villain he had accused of murder, and took to his bed with a plan to trap the sender into the belief that his box had succeeded in its fell purpose. Eventually the alarmed Mrs Hudson, came to me to say that Holmes was dying, and that he had brought back to Baker Street a disease caught during an investigation. This, she said, was on Thames-side, "at an alley in Rotherhithe." It did not occur to me at the time [as with hindsight, it should have done] to doubt this tale, for Holmes would never have confided such information to his landlady without some compelling motive, which was of course --as I sourly brooded over it later-- to deceive me!

That his stratagem worked did not lessen my chagrin at being so unscrupulously used, and my ensuing displeasure might have led to a longer separation than it did, but for the decision by the criminal, the infamous Culverton Smith, to end his own life in his remand cell with a dose of the potassium salt of hydrocyanic acid. The fatal crystals were delivered by his servant, who fled the country before he could be arrested. The hullabaloo in the London gutter press --which would stew in the following year in righteous fury over the failure of the official police to arrest 'Jack the Ripper,' the terror of London's East End-- gives some indication now of the professionally-damaging exposure I must have suffered from appearing in a sensational trial. This I bluntly pointed out to Holmes on a delayed visit to Baker Street, after he sent me a note brazenly chiding me for forsaking his company. Such gall he had! But then --and at once-- he was most profusely apologetic:

"I much regret that I should have abused your loyal friendship, my dear Watson, by allowing my detestation of Culverton Smith to draw me into what I admit was an ill-mannered deception as it applied to you. But I also deceived Mrs Hudson by encouraging her to believe that I had been investigating a case near the Surrey Docks when I was, by that time in fact, busy on the other bank of the River."

Imagine such brass if you can! I struggled to remain basilisk-like under a sly glance from my friend aimed at detecting, I believe, whether I was further irritated [as indeed I was] at having his playing on my deepest sensibilities so slightingly compared with his entirely-harmless practising upon his doting landlady, to whom one side of the Thames or the other could make not a scrap of difference. I must report with regret that my efforts at silent reproof went for nothing. I should not have expected otherwise of course: Holmes was as perfectly armoured as a Greek Fury in his ruthless pursuit of his natural quarry the evil-doer, and so, perfectly ruthlessly, he was certain to go on.

He laughed at me directly as he read my mind: "Even so, Watson, Culverton Smith would have had to wait for his come-uppance but for a turn that left me idle for some days awaiting the arrival of a ship coming up-Channel. And as it turns out, your welcome visit could not have been better timed, since there is pertinent news this very morning."

So it was that in the manner of the meeting or reunion I have outlined, I was helplessly swept back at once into the partnership with my dear friend Mr Sherlock Holmes. It continued with a sensational case of two brutish murders involving the official police on both sides of the English Channel, and the English community on the beautiful mountainous Atlantic island of Madeira, famous for its unique wine, but also the location of the so-called Hobson's Coal-Hole, a grimy coal-bunkering and fresh water station for steamships. The tentacles of the crimes were to extend to our own Thames shore in the infamous East London haunts that include, on Wapping Wall, the precincts of a once-notorious tavern known, curiously, as 'The Prospect of Whitby.' This investigation completed my crowded activity in the company of my famous friend in the later months of 1887, ending with the "Blue Carbuncle" case at Christmas. That I could write nothing of it before now, though I had excellent notes in my diary, was because of the interdict laid on my presentations by Holmes when he retired to his beekeeping on those Sussex green hills we perplex foreigners by calling Downs. I always stressed the sensational, he complained, and in doing so inevitably slighted the scientific reasoning of his method, which he would one day set forth in the planned great work of his own. Since that work never appeared, I believe it is right that I make the public aware, in certain strange criminal cases, of facts it can do no harm to publish.

~0~

"Oh, let us say nothing more about it, Holmes," I had ended

our parley, putting a tolerant smile and a shrug on some lingering shades of exasperation: You well know that I approve of your determination in the face of crime. I must admit that without my certainty that you were at death's door, I could not have carried off the part you wished me to play."

I had hardly finished this pompous exculpation before the world's untidiest consultant-detective was scrabbling about in the usual heap of prints tumbled about his chair. He enjoyed praise in a professional respect as merely his due but found it acutely embarrassing, I believe, to have it inextricably and openly alloyed with affection. With no trace of acknowledgement, therefore, for my pardon, the *Morning Post* for the previous day was handed over, already folded open to the relevant article. I was driven to the conclusion that he had allowed about twenty hours after the delivery of his note, and had watched with outrageous self-satisfaction my arrival at the hour he had calculated.

The item to which he referred was the first report in the shipping news column:

<u>"Scotland Yard man boards ship in mysterious</u>
<u>island murder case."</u>

The text continued: "An enterprising London inspector of police commandeered a fast-sailing pilot cutter in Dover Harbour yesterday to overhaul one of the biggest of our old but sturdy

Scarborough colliers. She was boarded as she made her way to round the Forelands into the North Sea on her return from Madeira Island and France. The coal carrier, a registered British ship at Loyd's, is strangely named *The Prospect of Whitby*. She was reported to have entered the Channel some days ago, but had not been reported to Lloyd's as having put in at any official harbour. That she did not approach the shore but still held her course when approaching the strait, caused Inspector Morton of Scotland Yard to hurry down to Dover. His mission was to investigate a report that a Frenchman suspected of murder in the English community on Madeira had taken passage in the collier to escape arrest.

"The Inspector, one of the Yard's upcoming younger generation of detectives, arrived in time to make his dramatic interception, but his zeal was to go unrewarded. The collier's captain reported that he had indeed taken a 'furriner' on board after discharging cargo at 'Hobson's Coal-Hole,' as the Madeira coaling station for steamers is commonly known. The man was uncommunicative and seemed to have little English, but still enough to make 'a grand palaver' on arrival in the Channel over his wish to be put ashore by boat on the French coast --at Honfleur, he insisted, which is at the very mouth of the Seine. The captain was only too pleased to agree to this time-saving convenience, which left him with no need to put in officially at any Channel port

7

before entering the North Sea. There he could make formal landfall at his usual loading port of Newcastle, where he could also have some weather damage made good.

"The captain would not undertake to confirm that his passenger was certainly French, or even to describe his appearance: the man kept his head wrapped in scarves or a blanket against the weather, which had become seasonally 'a bit brisk but rightly serviceable.' To this bluff seaman, his passenger seemed 'half-blind,' because he wore thick blue glasses much too big for him, held precariously aboard his nose with one hand while using the other to keep himself attached to the ship. He knew nothing, he told Morton, of the allegation that his passenger had murdered a trader in the harbour at Funchal [the capital town of Madeira]. He would never have let such a villain into his ship, he declared, if he knew of any crime being held against him. In this way, as Morton complained to your correspondent, his suspect had 'skipped off safe' into France.

"Scotland Yard has passed on its quest to the French police, providing the suspect's identity from the ship's manifest --given as Roger Dileel, native of Marseilles-- though there is little hope in the present state of unrest in Paris that anything will be done to find the suspect. The case is truly the primary business of the Portuguese authorities, who are in at least nominal command of

Madeira, but it is understood that our Police entertain little hope of receiving meaningful assistance from the Authorities in Lisbon."

Reciting this case history Holmes spread the bony fingers of both hands, patting them together two by two and tip to tip: "So there you have it, Watson, the enterprising official policeman had no luck. He was smart enough, however to call here directly from St. Paul's Station on his return last night, to thank me for so nearly having put him in the way of making a useful arrest."

At this, I lodged a mild and [I have to admit] somewhat mischievously dismissive protest: "Really now, Holmes, you must know that you are leaving me quite in the dark, even as you drown me in this flood of information! I am most curious to learn how you have managed to involve yourself in such a minor case as the killing of a poor coalman in Madeira."

Holmes responded warmly and quite waspishly to this gentle provocation: "Even you my dear Watson, in your pragmatic style, could hardly have ignored a murder case with so intriguing a location as 'Hobson's Coalhole' and a flight by sea in a ship mystifyingly called *The Prospect of Whitby,* but it is no poor coalman with whom I have become involved, even if two minor figures in the coal trade, rather than one, have paid with their lives. You know that it is not with me a matter of much money, even if there is a *rich* 'coal man' in the case --I suppose you will call him that in your sensationalized accounts-- wealthy enough to have sent me a long and costly telegram. He reports that the Funchal victim had become a minor shareholder in his coal lighterage company, but as little more than a tallyman, publicly, when he sold out, for commercial paper, to the more successful enterprises owned by my client on the waterfront of Madeira and, less notably, Spanish Grand Canary. All the details of the case so far depend on the telegraph, Watson. In the ordinary way, I would refuse to touch it."

"A telegram does not seem to me much of a hurdle over which to leap for your professional services in a case of murder, Holmes."

"Aha, but there I must fault you again, my dear fellow: this telegram came by the under-sea cable at a cost [when first I heard of it] approaching one gold sovereign per word. It can take a whole minute to transmit only half-a-dozen words. For some business interests that can be little to pay for vital information or important news. I am confident that, for my endeavours, this price marks a new peak in the scientific struggle against crime."

To this example of the rare pedantic humour of my friend, I could not resist a return shaft in kind: "Shall you long persist, then, Holmes, in leaving me also in this matter almost entirely under water?"

The fingertip patting ended with a scowl and a distinct sniff, followed by more scrabbling in the back of the sofa: ending, eventually, in production of the costly document. It was handed over with something of a flourish, I thought, and for a reason made instantly obvious:

"To the Most Honourable Mr Sherlock Holmes," it began, "Master of Science of Criminal Detection, and Famous Scourge of Law Breakers in the British Empire of Baker Street, London."

I was unable to suppress a chuckle at these lavish honorifics and awkward syntax, and could not resist remarking to my friend that he should not allow himself to feel *embarrassed* by this costly form of address, worth five or six pounds Sterling for a start, since he must be aware that such *odious fulsomeness* passed for mere politeness in some quarters of the British Realm.

For that dripping sarcasm, I was pounced upon at once: "The colony of Madeira is not a part of the Empire if that is what you mean, Watson; it belongs to Portugal. As for the somewhat flowery form of address, it has perhaps become customary there, even among British business residents. There is a substantial English population, with its own church and well-filled graveyard and, importantly, substantial trading businesses in wine and imported staples --and lately in coal for steamships. I have learned that wine and coal have made the family of the present Mr Hobson very respectable and very rich, though the business began with practically nothing. And as you will note from the form, he is now also the official agent for the submarine cable concern, and may well qualify on that account for a cheaper rate. But I shall save you from wading through more of his *odious* compliments, and tell you essentially why the telegram interests me:

"There have been two particularly brutal crimes involving the Hobson businesses: one in Madeira, the other in Puerto de la Luz, in the Canary Islands --which is a more loosely-organized and mixed colony belonging to Spain.

"The attack in Madeira, not surprisingly, involved a coal hammer, and --very surprisingly to me-- a ship's boiler-room coal rake, a long-handled and long-toothed forged iron tool. I have established that such rakes, very heavy in the head, are often sold by bunkering yards. They are required to be massive enough to sink the working end through a bed of burning coals to drag out soft clumps of near-molten clinker which would otherwise clog the fire grate. The professional coal hammer is rather like a bill hook but with a hammer head on the back of a blade. The blade enables the tool to be used to *split* a block of coal, or, as this case, a skull.

"The owner of the skull appears to have been the French owner and manager of a failing coal yard bought out by Mr Henry Hobson in exchange for value --no money changed hands-- in the shape of non-negotiable shares in Hobson's group of companies.

The yard still traded as Boulanger and Company, of Rouen, and was still directed by the former owner, Monsieur Marcel Boulanger. According to Mr Hobson, Boulanger was found dead, lying on his back on the floor of the yard's office by labourers returning to work in the morning. Mr Hobson writes that the poor fellow's face was an unrecognizable ruin of smashed flesh and facial bone, though his skull, clean-shaven against the ever-present coal dust, showed only a single cleaving blow, a killing stroke I do not doubt, from the blade of the coal hammer. But the rake, horribly fouled, was cast upon the floor with its head close to the dead man. In keeping with the common practice in hotter climes, this terrible corpse was hurried to the grave before sunset.

"The suspect in the case is thought to be also a Frenchman, who sailed for England at first light on the morning after the murder. This was the passenger whom Inspector Morton, acting on my hint, had intended to interview and perhaps arrest at the head of the Channel. He had passed some days in Madeira, where he was accepted in Funchal, a friendly capital, as a visitor newly-arrived from the Canaries, travelling in the Atlantic islands for the sake of his health. He went about in nondescript brown or grey, loose and cool garments, with his head shrouded in dark wraps or mufflers. His eyes were always shielded by blue or smoked 'blinkers,' as our client calls them, in the belief that they keep out light which would otherwise trouble weak eyes from the sides. It occurs to me that the criminal probably waited until he was certain of an immediate passage out of the island before carrying out his crime. That would seem to chime with the sea captain's avowals.

"Mr Hobson's only suggestion of motive is the possibility of revenge for some past business offence. He may be right, of course, and this matter of motive is particularly crucial to an inquiry in which you and I Watson are making history by depending on an amateur's assessment of the site and circumstances for a start, and that transmitted by wires. It must have been a very serious business offence --if that is what it was-- yet our client, long in the same business, knows nothing of it. He is careful to note details he suggests may be significant, however: such as that the coal wharf area is deserted by early evening unless a lighter is actually being loaded for a ship coaling in the bay; a spare key to the yard hanging on an unhidden hook in the yard shed, gates to the yard left secured by padlocked chain, accessible from inside or out so that the body would certainly be found by the labourer who first climbed the gate and looked for the key in the unlocked shed in the morning. An arrangement to stop anyone from blundering through the yard into the harbour --in darkness or drink-- thus made sure that the whole town quickly heard of the crime, says our client.

"He also tells us that the visiting seeker after health was one of the few who quickly become familiar in Funchal itself. Such visitors, sometime guests of the wealthier families, are usually met at the pier and whisked off to private estates. Our visitor stayed in the town, where Monsieur Boulanger's sale of his yard to Mr Hobson was no secret."

Here, Holmes suddenly paused in this exposition, his eyes shifting unseeingly in the exaggeratedly deep sockets of his aquiline face, but in that unfocused fashion I had seen on occasion, often with his violin bow in hand, denoting that some fresh review of information impended. But after a minute or two for reflection, my friend picked up his thread again:

"Mr Hobson goes on to give us very little history in the case of a cowardly attack on a son he sent a few months ago to manage a much less important small coal depot he acquired at Las Palmas, on Grand Canary Island. He mentions this yard, much run down he says, only because it was pressed into their bargain by Boulanger. He accepted it to give full effect to a determination by the Frenchman to abandon his waterfront properties for a share in Hobson's various successful businesses.

"The young man was attacked by footpads after dark, walking home in rural surroundings. The ruffians stole his gold watch and a valuable jewelled fob he had been advised not to wear in public.

They almost succeeded in kicking him to death, but were driven off by a party of fishermen passing on the way to their night's work. The young fellow is too damaged to have long to live. Hobson believes the ruffians were paid but offers no reasoning for the belief. You Watson will have no difficulty in your soft-hearted way in understanding him: he sent a son to attend to a run-down business he had accepted almost as a matter of charity [to hear him tell of it] and so must be seen as bringing about the young man's death. That is hard to contemplate. I believe it is, nevertheless, a part of our case: a riddle within a riddle. In solving one, we'll solve the other.

"Our historic witness by telegraph adds that his family's businesses in the Atlantic islands have a reputation for honest dealing and for fair treatment of their hired labour. It has not been difficult for me to confirm that this is so. In Madeira they are honoured for an earlier Hobson's risking ruin to save the island's famous wine industry when disease destroyed the native vines, and dealers were abandoning the island. That repute stands true today here in London also --mainly in the wine trade with its irreplaceable butts of Malmsey or Madeira. There are also some reputable members of the family established at home here in England, connected but little concerned practically with the conduct of affairs in the Atlantic islands, and in no way adversely affected by the crimes in Funchal and Las Palmas.

"There exists in the trade here the vague suggestion --an echo we may call it-- of a political cause of violence such as is not uncommon in the public affairs of France, at home or abroad: this I gather from London newspaper citations of Paris reports aimed at the wealth and ambitions of a power-seeking extended family named Boulanger. I have established that there is such a business at Rouen, also widely engaged in trade in ships' coal, and builders' lime. As you must know, the city is also on the River Seine, not far from the sea. It is sometimes referred to as 'the port of Paris' and hired watermen could have landed a fugitive there from Honfleur in a few hours on the flood . Boulanger is far from being an uncommon name, of course . . . in France they do have a violent history to do with bread. But coal, Watson? Coal for Paris . . . "

Holmes's voice trailed off into another meditative silence --seeming so, I thought again, because he felt unsure in this marshalling of the limited information at his disposal, and inability to interview a subject or throw himself down with his glass and snoop out the clues for himself 'from the ground up,' as it were, and from his first principles. But I considered myself quite my friend's equal in mundane political matters and did not hesitate to offer helpful opinion:

"I see it as very likely Holmes, indeed I do, that the French today include many thousands of highly conservative people willing to spend money to hound any business owned by others suspected of being linked with their troublesome General Georges Boulanger. It is a damned serious affair, Holmes --to us quite unimaginable. He is alleged to be rallying regiments of 'loyal' French willing to support a Napoleonic *solution* [as he calls it] to France's problems, in a coup against their shaky Republican Government. Those gentlemen seem to have made themselves the latest of the world's masters in such matters as stimulating outbreaks of violence and the general hounding of scapegoats."

My friend, master in the theory and practice of criminality, greeted my second-hand distillations from French public opinion with a thin smile. They were coolly dismissed: "That is certainly one of the elementary first approximations possible Watson, but quite excessively sweeping for our circumstances. I think a political solution is far from essential to the understanding of this case, as I shall explain to you. First, however, I must make further use of the wires myself for two or three urgent messages. If you are free and not averse to visiting France, perhaps you would be good enough to look up tomorrow's train and ferry timetables for a brief expedition to Rouen."

To this request he added a muttered rumination, addressed it seemed, to the air of the sitting room. "It seems that I must hurry back to the River."

Aha! Holmes might aspire to be effective at once on both sides of a single river, but not even he could be at one time beside two capital waterways on either side of the Channel! With this puerile rag of consolation I did as he wished, and confess to doing so without demur -- more shame upon me for that, since my Mary had become so soon unsurprised to be left alone suddenly and indefinitely. In her frank way, she had become skilled at directing callers to one or two trusted colleagues who had [I believe] come to regard *my* rounds as contributing frequently to *their* incomes. As only a quite ordinary general practitioner with a modest allowance for some Eastern Service time to his credit, I would have no-one imagine that the pecuniary loss occasioned to me in handing over fees to *locums* was made up for by sales of published accounts of my adventures with Holmes. Far from it! Nor did I enjoy the prospect of a hurried trip to France alone, which I took to be the meaning of Holmes's request for train times to Portsmouth and sailings to LeHavre, the ferry port for Rouen, while he needs must hurry only so far as Wapping --insalubrious though that East London dockland must be. Nevertheless, I found the required information before going home to make preparations for departure, leaving Holmes scratching at his telegram forms for the Buttons to take to the post office. I did not return to Baker Street until late next morning, when I found my friend still pecking at a breakfast of buttered eggs, and wafting off the crumbs of Mrs Hudson's hot bread that sprinkled the morning's society chatter, police news and criminal court columns from which he drew much of the information to be filed in his great Index. [That treasure I believe to have been shamefully discarded by his brilliant but idle elder brother Mycroft, who would certainly have regarded it as a collection of ephemeral trivia entirely unworthy of his care or room in his house. Cloister, I should say, since he spent so little time in public pursuits.]

"Ah, there you are Watson," said Homes, affecting not to have noticed my surprise, "with valise, long greatcoat and umbrella. The regular officer prepared to travel utterly dependably, come what may, if not exactly incognito. Excellent! I, as you see, may well need obvious defence against the lower denizens of our meanest streets. But I have news from France already this morning that must disappoint by depriving you of a visit to Rouen. I regret it, but it may help to soothe Mrs Watson, who will not be troubled by visions of her gallant husband actually running worse risks in the East End. I did not see Rouen when travelling but it is said to have a fine statue of Joan of Arc, who was executed there for encouraging expression of the discontent that has since been nurtured into a French traditional passion; but then [*slyly*] you have

20

made yourself an expert in such matters already, Watson. The Saint has also been freely painted, but today we are to follow in the footsteps of Mr Whistler and Mr Turner." He handed over a telegram that lay by his plate and got to his feet. I must confess that my eyebrows rose and my chin dropped appreciably [which by this time in our association it had no right to do] as I took my next breath. I beheld Holmes in the stained and rumpled smock of a messier exponent of the Fine Arts, now fixing a vast silk bow at his neck and pulling on to dangle over his right ear one of those flopping-soft black berets affected by painters indoors or out. From his left ear there depended a large gold ring. Thus embellished, he might well need a guardian in the Eastern stews of London, but I refused to feed his ego by admiring the disguise, when I could not help but feel hugely uncomfortable at the prospect of appearing in public in association with such a vision. I turned wordlessly to the telegram. It read:

"Boulanger Rouen depot of lime and coal functions since 1862 to prosper in coal plenty of this day. [Didier] Boulanger Père died since three months after inspection of family commerce overseas. Madame Boulanger and only daughter --Mlle Garance, not-married lady of mature years-- rest in command of the simple commerce, but Madame is judged too frail and soon to be lost to this world. Eldest son, Marcel and next brother, Jules, reputed holding two companion family tradings since years six, seven, for engine coals. Marcel believed to La Madeira and Jules to Londres. Also may exist twin boys, more youngs, Henri and Louis, sent from La France since many years to look to business in Canary Islands by cause of ill favours in public impressions for eyes of pink and more presentations in albinism. Thank you in your request." This message was signed by one Georges-Pierre Latouche, Lloyd's agent at Le Havre and Rouen.

Holmes continued: "The other telegrams are from Inspector Morton, who is pleased to know where to find me in the next few days if need be, and who also undertakes to seek information from the prefecture of police in Rouen concerning property of the late Boulanger, Senior, on the Seine waterfront. That is an open matter if I am right in my discounting of   possibilities. I am not much impressed by the prosperity, if that is the word, of the Boulanger businesses. How impressed can one be about an enterprise left in the hands of a mature spinster who must care for her failing mother? There is also a letter from a consulting engineer in the business of building marine boilers. He is kind enough to supply the approximate dimensions of rakes used in the handling of steam coal in ships' furnaces. They are not garden rakes other than in the general shape of rakes as we know them, and would be of no service even in a coal yard: but it seems that they are a stock item for supply to ships with which to draw clinker from boiler furnaces. He has secured a drawing and points out some details: these rakes can be as much as eight to ten feet long, to reach deep into a firebox heating the tubes of a boiler long enough to flash cold water into superheated steam. Rock impurities in the coal melt into clinker, which must be raked from the fire grate. Such a rake cannot be used to strike in a confined space. It is not suitable there as a murder weapon. There is also another message from the under-sea cable, in which Mr Hobson responds with the detailed dimensions of the office in the coal-yard hutch. Those limits govern what will serve for a murder weapon, particularly in respect of ceiling height. You may recall my telling you of a client accused of murder in a cellar in which there was no room to swing the *felling* axe he was alleged to have used to chop off his victim's head.

"In this case it seems clear enough to me, that the hatchet side of the coal hammer was used for the killing --hence the cleft in the skull. But the rake was employed. It was used like a long heavy hoe, but at full stretch, to destroy the victim's features beyond ready recognition while keeping the attacker's garments unstained. But now we must lose no time shifting ourselves to the coal holes of Wapping Wall. I also have a bag packed and these borrowed impedimenta you see strapped up." He indicated a folding easel

23

and a box of paints.

"It is just as well to go armed, Watson," he agreed affably, reading my mind after we had loaded his paraphernalia and settled into a hansom for the visit to that sorry end of London where human life teems for no better reason than to serve the commerce of the great docks, and where it is still not unusual to find the less fortunate and sicker teeming ones dead drunk, or simply dead, in the gutters.

A nod was enough to satisfy Holmes. But what former officer would have travelled to an unknown part of France at such a time of ferment without his life-tested and trusted service revolver? I was even less willing to be diverted from pressing my famous friend for information if there was a possibility of being exposed to violence calling for gunfire. I felt bound to insist: Why were we going to Wapping Wall, one of our Great Wen's most disreputable stretches of riverside? I did not put it quite so bluntly as that, knowing that Holmes would fence unless he was certain of his ground: I would receive the tiresome lecture beginning *You know my methods, Watson. We must find the one solution, however surprising, that cannot be ruled out.*

"May I know, Holmes, what, perhaps, you expect to discover at Wapping Wall and what led you there?"

Our hansom was rattling, in the customary fashion caused by

the granite-cobbles notorious in these accounts and those of other scribes. [How long before we can be rid of these stones?] We were at the foot of Ludgate Hill before I received some sort of answer, for Holmes might as well have lapsed into a trance once he had satisfied himself in the matter of artillery.

"It's 'The Prospect of Whitby,' Watson." He came suddenly to life: "It is in my Index as one species of centre found in criminal history, satisfying the need of certain kinds of lawbreakers for safe harbour; this one much benefited from the nearness of Execution Dock when hanging was a public spectacle, and with having been the hostelry of choice of the most feared judge of his day: Hanging Jeffries. It burned down at least twice when it was a thieves' den known as the Devil's Tavern. One might expect that such a refuge could hardly exist openly now, in our enlightened times, but I have established that Pepys and Dickens were not alone in supping there for no better reasons than idle sensation. But some of the stews and mews around the house have fallen down or been pulled down in recent years to make way for coal yards. The tavern took its name, strangely, not from any aspect of the port of Whitby but from the name of the ship. This ship was simply named *The Prospect*, I imagine. *Of Whitby*, then referred to her home port, in a customary fashion. I hope we shall encounter her, since she is often to be found on her own mooring at Wapping, and not on the other bank as I first thought. She regularly loads coal in Newcastle, sometimes splitting her cargo between London and Rouen and, as we now know, taking loads even as far as Madeira in season.

"We are to stay at the inn, Watson, where we are expected as convivial country travellers, one devoted to --I will not say painting-- applying colours ground in oil to stretched canvas. That is very far behind the specialists known to have painted views from the inn backyard, but not out of keeping with Wapping Wall.

"I shall do a bit of that sufficient to establish my *bona fides*, but turn to street scenes about the coal yards. And here we are Watson! *The Prospect of Whitby!* Behold the typical public house daub of the type of ship in which our mysterious Frenchman fled from Madeira. He may well have had a rough and wet passage in such a low tub, don't you think?"

On a single glance at this heavy-laden sailing vessel I found it easy to shiver in agreement, but the innkeeper, forewarned by telegram, had rooms set aside for us with welcome fires in the grates. He proved staunchly uncommunicative when asked about any recent visitor --a point on which Holmes [genuinely, I believe] complimented him for defending the confidentiality of a guest who, said the landlord, gave no trouble and said little, did not complain about English food or the wine, and paid his bill promptly and without question.

The inn's resident head potman, made oppositely confidential by Sterling coin of the realm, was praised instead for his powers of observation, shocking Holmes by letting slip that "there was a strange frog 'ere your honour. I can smell 'em. Nothing would he take but brandy and water; tasted our wine and swore by one o' their saints I never 'eard tell of, as 'ow it were terrible stuff set aside in 'is 'ome country as fit only for our English tavern trade. And this, mark you ginlmen, from one of the most 'orrible customers I ever clapped me mincepies on --never come out of 'is room without 'avin' 'is 'ead all wrapped up in mufflers, and wi' thick smoked glasses tied on in a bandage. He paid 'is bill orl right, but daily so's 'e could run any time --this bein' a inn, we'd else o' kept 'is baggage, see? But 'e never come back fer 'is washin.' The washerwoman even looked fer 'im. Any'ow, he never 'eard anythin' from me about all what 'e wanted to know every time 'e opened 'is mouth: Was there any Frenchman in trade 'ereabouts, 'appen runnin' a coalyard?"

Could the uncollected washing be inspected? Holmes asked. He was always looking for decent rags for painting, he explained, noting my sudden concentration on details of the worn stone flagging of the ground floor and smiling at me like brass.

But nothing was going to stop the potman : "Lor' bless you sir, Martha will 'ave sold 'is slops by now --seeing as she wasn't to be paid fer washing 'em."

But Martha, summoned by whatever serves for grapevine on Wapping Wall, and being assured by the Queen's Head on a shilling that she was not to be accused of stealing by false laundering, disclosed that a shirt involved "wasn't English-made, sir, but I don't say I'd know where it was stitched over --an' I've seen all sorts 'avin bin at the washin' sin' a girl--'tis no bad trade to be at hereabouts on account of the seacoal yards. I swear 'tis in the very wells, the dratted dust flies all over. I'm not sayin' I'd as soon be without it, mind; 'twould be a ill wind for any washerwoman as blowed it all away. But that ol' Potty 'as told you wrong sir, for I did let the ragman 'ave the genlmn's unmentionables, but I a'nt sold the shirt. Rare beautiful that is. The ragman would've cheated me for it, an' if I didn't take 'is price he wun't never ave took nuffink else, devil take '*im*, ferevermore."

"Half a crown for it! cried Holmes, generously but starting up a haggling, nevertheless, by this excess of enthusiasm in the form of coin --eventually securing the mysterious garment, in tuppeny increments of wheedling, at three shillings and fourpence with two days' laundry for two visitors thrown into the bargain. "But it will never fit you nor yet your friend!" said the washerwoman, with all the authority of a thousand shirts washed and flat-ironed.

"Oh, it's not for me," declared Holmes, switching his story

without batting an eyelid. "I intend to give it back to its owner if I can find him. He must be sad to lose such a fine piece of French needlework."

"You'll not find that too hard, sir, wiv a shillin' or two --being a ginelmun and 'avin,' such good Christian reasons. Try the sailors' lodgins, sir. They'll know where 'e is -- if 'e's still 'ereabouts. But beggin' your pardon, sir, if that's French work, I'm a-robbin' you. 'Tis far finer than them wicked Napoleums ever did."

~0~

"I fear we are too late, Watson," declared Holmes, looking as down in the mouth as I have seen him.

We were back at the inn where, after a dinner of chops and a wretched pease pottage, he was going over the embroidery on the shirt with his powerful glass.

"Too late?" I cried, now exasperated beyond my poor patience. "Holmes: For what are we too late?"

"Well you may ask Watson. It is for the truth of which I am now less certain. Yet I am sure there are the makings of another killing signified in this beautiful work under my hand."

"Oh, come now, Holmes. You are already sure that your rich client was right to set up the hue and cry if an albino Frenchman murdered one of his elder brothers. That albino was traced back to France. Now we hear that a Frenchman afflicted by albinism, surely the murderer's twin, has been here on probably a counterpart expedition, this one to kill Jules Boulanger the other elder brother in the family. I can see a clear motive: they were deprived of the use of a yard in the Canary islands in which they scraped out a living, and will stop at nothing, including murders, to recoup by seizing their brothers' businesses in Madeira and here in Wapping."

"My dear Watson! Pray do look again at this merchant's shirt worn --as you now propose-- by a poor devil in the coal business who fled from the site of a grisly killing he perpetrated: this garment with its stitching and embroidery so fine that a washerwoman accustomed to serve travellers for years had never seen its like. It doesn't make sense, does it?"

To that I had no answer; Holmes took to his token painting and sketching about the inn that same afternoon lugging the same 'canvas' from one spot to another he wished to observe. My job was simply to keep the curious at such a distance as to disguise the fact that Holmes lacked any shred of talent with crayon and brush. An evening outing found several sailors' lodgings at which the fancy shirt was exhibited, to no effect other than exclamations about its beauty, Silver shillings, thinly spread, produced interest next day, but it was interest in the prospect of more shillings: no certain information about seemingly near-blind men going about with their heads swaddled and eyes hidden by blue or dark brown 'bottle bottoms.' I found the hunting among the dockland hovels every bit as disgusting as I expected: many humans living in hovels unfit even to confine pigs. It is well known that they exist still in the mews of Marylebone, not a stone's throw from Baker Street, where 'upstairs' costers share space with their 'downstairs' ponies. They are the sturdy "better-off" kind who can afford painted carts and horse brass. For the poorer, who *share* spaces built for animals, life is grim, and only disease is certain. But all these are as kings and queens compared with the inhabitants of our ancient docklands. It is to the credit of the black trade in seacoals that rows of their grim hovels have been broken down into heaps of rubbish and burned. It was the remaining vermin-ridden stews and several abandoned and ruined yards that Holmes and I hunted over, and where, when Holmes was about to give up his posing for the day, there came a discovery more surprising and baffling than any before, though I do not make too much of it, since it occurred in my rôle merely as a hired guard:

Holmes had selected a pitch with a view of a yard in which a couple of labourers loaded sacks of coal for a waiting horse and cart, a closed and barred gate on its left and --on the right in our view-- an abandoned yard with one leaf of its gate missing and the other, hanging outward on one hinge, forced well back against the outside of the front fence. I shooed off some street urchins and poked my head into this gateway in which a stack of battered and broken willow coal baskets competed for interest with a heap of unsellable coal dust piled in open view. A massive broad shovel of the road-mender's type was thrust into this pile, the shaft broken off at the handle. We had seen several such heaps in anonymous and abandoned yards, but idle curiosity caused me to step back and look behind the half gate --practically immovable as it was with its bottom hinge broken. There were two words to be seen from the difficult angle, crudely rendered in once-white paint, grey-blotched by exposure to emissions of sulphuretted fumes from wet coal, acting on that equally-harmful white acetate of lead which cumulatively poisons our professional house painters. The words were:

ANGER

[and]

USE NUTS

Holmes saw at once, of course, that "anger" was roughly half of "Boulanger," but remained unamused by the suggestion contained in the second half-line. which I [having been domesticated] guessed to be what was left of "Best house nuts" or, perhaps, "Boilerhouse nuts."

Clearly, we had found the yard or a former yard of the French elder brother, Jules Boulanger, who had come years before from Rouen. But where was he? It was galling that Holmes, though generously expressing himself pleased with my discovery, spent little time inspecting the pile of coal dust after taking up the broken shovel and dragging away from its edge a thick band of small coal --fine pieces, a little larger or smaller than peas, that roll down when one makes a heap of any similar material, such as the mixed sand and gravel commonly used for garden paths. This I took to indicate that he recognized the disposition of the bits as showing that the stack had not been built in one task to hide a body. The stack of coal baskets also failed to take up little of his time --that devoted to a close examination of the black surface close about it, which showed no sign of recent disturbance.

I fell into fitful sleep eventually that night, disturbed by the sound of lashing rain with occasional claps of thunder making rest hard to find. My bed, comfortless to begin with, became heavy-laden with baskets of coal, pressed down to a few inches of freeboard in short seas under fierce squalls of loud and wet north-east wind . . . I felt my pillow shudder at each blow under bluff bows from that violent short chop which has sunk or driven on to shifting sands so many coastal cargo carriers, including several of those tasked with keeping London choking under pea soup-yellow fog. I felt the jolting progress in my bad shoulder and woke to find Holmes hissing at my ear and shaking me none too gently by the light from a hurricane lantern. "Hurry and dress, Watson; we must get back to that damned coalyard. I sensed there was something badly amiss there but have only now understood--"

He broke off when he noticed my rueful grimace as I grasped the shoulder with the opposite hand:

"Ah, my apologies Watson: Unforgivably careless of me, my dear fellow!"

The courtesies having been summarily offered for the unthinking awaking, he galloped on:

"The baskets, Watson! The pile of dust might as well have been thrown straight into my eyes."

The night had only a sliver of moon to spread over a limitless blackness. There were scudding clouds high aloft with this pale illumination, but little wind to stir the heavy damp along the river, and no sound as we sneaked back, by the flickering light of a one-candle lantern, to the site of the afternoon's discovery. Holmes held out an arm to bar the way as we neared the gap with the broken-down gate, taking out a taper the better to see the marks where his easel and chair had bitten into the coal and clay ground. Our footprints were easily picked out in an eerie reversal of the common procedure in which Holmes would be illuminating the prints of the villain in a case. But close to and narrowly crossing some of these marks for which we were responsible, there now stretched a broad set of shallow streaks marking the dragging of the uneven surface of something heavy. This track emerged from the gates, closed but unlocked, of the yard from which we had seen coal sacks gathered to be loaded on a cart. Within the yard we had investigated no change could we see. The pile of coal dust displayed the record of Holmes's poking with the broken shovel but lay otherwise undisturbed as did the stack of decrepit willow baskets, in a pyramid higher than the fence. Wordlessly, Holmes returned to the tracks outside and flung up the balanced wooden bar on the closed gates. One man to each leaf, we dragged them open enough to let us squeeze into the yard in which we had seen men working only a few hours before.

The early false dawn light was now enough to show walls of coal baskets stacked three-high, one within another, and ranged in double rows along both sides of the yard . . . but with three or four dragged aside --where they had concealed a gap open to the back of the stack of empty baskets in the yard alongside.

"Simple hide-hole built for the purpose, Watson" : Holmes pointed to a few planks inserted to keep the upper baskets steady when the lower ones were pulled out. "And I'll wager that unless he is actively involved in this case, the owner of this business knows nothing about it. You'll note how little coal remains at the back there; all these baskets will be pulled out to be returned when the next delivery comes in off the river, and that must be very soon. Make what you can of it, Watson."

"Well, Holmes, I would hazard that the need for this secret storage arose suddenly and recently, and --in view of what you have said-- may be about to disappear in the same manner as all these baskets we see. Quite why this should be, I cannot even a guess."

"Very good, Watson --and ingenious, wouldn't you say? Apparently, the yard is not usually locked, and, unlike that of the yard next-door, its surface is often disturbed in the course of business. You could have added, however, that this arrangement is the creation of an author who knows this immediate district intimately, that he has not had to deal with such a situation before and expects not to deal with its like again for the purpose of hiding the subject of a sudden death. Therefore, he makes no further effort to hide his hiding place. But there are three candidates. The missing basket, I'll surmise for the time being, has been housing the body of one, and first we must find it. For that task we cannot now do better than telegraph Inspector Morton at Scotland Yard. Since there is no time to be lost, Watson, I'll take a walk to the Wapping Post Office and send the message myself. Do you be so good, if you will, as to return to the inn and keep watch on the quay."

In this way it was that I strolled into one of the shocks of my unofficial career, as I fancied it, as something of a Boswell to Holmes's Johnson.

The quiet inn yard overlooking the river was crowded even so early, with carters and a rougher-looking crew of longshoremen and "wharfies" [some with wicked looking marlinspikes thrust in their belts, and rope slings at least twenty feet long folded over their shoulders, with strange flattened double hooks at both ends] --all these attendants already well fuelled with cheap drink, and hollering to make themselves heard over the hubbub.

One surprise followed another: for beyond the low-water mark, a ship was being hove up snug to a permanent mooring post. *The Prospect of Whitby* had come in. She lay loaded heavily enough to take her deck down, as it seemed to me, perilously low: little more than a foot of freeboard over the tide. Before she was moored some sailors were already hauling heavy timbers off her hatches.

The third shock was to see the river's edge of Wapping Wall covered with coal baskets stacked three or four high, scores of them. One of them --Holmes being right-- holding a corpse.

But where was Holmes, and what was to be done?

In the emergency, as I foolishly thought it to be, I hurried to Holmes's room in the inn to take up a sketch book and a stump of crayon; with these I lounged in full view on a rear balcony high above water to keep count of baskets going aboard and intending to note anything suspicious. A few minutes later an empty hansom cab turned on the edge of the inn yard and dashed away back along Wapping Wall. Holmes came round the rear corner in company with a man in those plain clothes that make a policeman instantly recognizable, and, moments later and more particularly, recognizable to me as Inspector Morton of Scotland Yard. In such company, Holmes the pantomime painter looked even more disreputable than he had done in mine. Perhaps it was Morton's ill-fitting but shining clean suit and lack of an umbrella. I threw down the sketch book and crayon to hurry down, feeling [quite inexplicably] put out.

"Ah, there you are Watson," said the arch-enemy of crime, briskly rubbing his hands: "I told the Inspector you had remained on guard duty."

"Indeed, Holmes? I was beginning to think that I should have been with you in that capacity!"

"Oh, my special-rate message went through almost immediately to the Yard, Watson. There, Morton had it at once and so replied --that he would stop at the Post Office and kindly collect me. I had time only to find a tobacconist and restock our supply of ship's shag. But I see now that we have plenty of time . . ."

"My pleasure to find you here, Doctor," said Morton, butting in to offer a firm hand, and stifle any further acid remarks from me. At once he was for getting to business:

"Have you seen anything you think suspicious, Doctor?"

"No, Inspector, I have not, but I have made a couple of observations about the unloading of these baskets into or out from those small flat-bottomed lighters, you see waiting. The baskets are lifted and lowered in stacks; two at a time filled with coal and, I imagine, three or four together as mere bulk when empty, stacked ready as you see. You'll note that the handles are lined up from top to bottom. The hooked ends of those slings you see are passed, from top to bottom, through the handles. --Those doubled opposite-facing hooks, which a carter told me are called sisters, drop through the stacked handles and are closed opposite to each other on the lowest. As long as there is some little load on the hoist the hooks remain locked. At the delivery end the load is let off, the sisters are parted from the basket handles, drop shut beside each other, and are whisked out free, leaving the tower of baskets standing, or standing two and two side by side coming or going. It is simple but ingenious really: A way of closing ladies neck chains works here in heavy industry: and nobody actually manhandles as much as one basket of coal! This use of stacks works in our favour also --unless three nested empty baskets plus one containing only a corpse stand just as high as four baskets, but--"

"It may be quicker"--

Morton's rude intervention was kindly cut short by Holmes, who could be diplomatically deaf when it suited him: "An excellent piece of observation, Watson. What you have discovered means that we can probably spot the victim in the case --if, ah, he should still be substantial enough-- without warning off any concerned watcher who happens to be here also. Would you not agree, Morton?"

The Inspector was enabled to look owlish when he could have looked foolish, but became embarrassing in agreement, pressing a second shaking of hands and murmuring, "Excellent, yes, excellent, Doctor." However, a shortcoming of my "watching" proposal, glaringly obvious as I thought of it, soon became evident: the working of the ship was to go on day and night! Holmes was unperturbed:

"If you draw a vertical section through a couple of these baskets, my dear Watson, one perched within the other, you will find that they do not fit very closely. Recall how they appeared at that coal yard. I doubt we shall find a body by eyeing the nested baskets. We may find our party, however, by watching for someone who will be relieved to know that a corpse is safely stowed aboard *The Prospect of Whitby*. You must now admit the practicality of my outfit, since I can sit and you can pretend to protect me while I pretend to paint --a *nocturne* perhaps, to illustrate this unusual chapter in the annals of crime. But I must prevail upon our good Inspector here to avoid prominence --other than as an admirer of this daubing-- until the moment comes to make an arrest. The ship must get off her assigned load here enough to give working space in the hold before these waiting baskets can be started down from the wharf, and we do not know yet that they are all here."

I listened to Holmes --no-one more attentively-- as dockmen and sailors worked into their accustomed rhythm to swing out stacked baskets of coal --streaming dust like smoke-- into the waiting lighters lying docile on tide-top water, black and still. This was the signal for the potman and his boy to emerge from the inn loaded with trays bearing jugs of antidote fourpenny porter. The existence of a wider interest in these proceedings was demonstrated within the hour by a clatter of. heavy hooves signalling the arrival and unloading of two more cartloads of empty baskets. One cart joined a line beginning to form along Wapping Wall; the other rumbled away, only to return with a few more baskets before joining the waiting rank. At this, Morton spoke up again:

"I can't honestly say that I enjoy your artist work, Mister Holmes. I suppose it to be some of the modern stuff I am not qualified to judge. But you have made your case about the baskets and wagons, and so I'll risk the wait with you. But I'll be in difficulty at the Yard, indeed I shall, if I come back with another blank on a case about the murder of a Frenchman in a foreign country. I have no body yet, nor a name for the suspect the Frogs won't croak over, and not even a hint of a motive!"

"Oh, I can help you with better than that, Inspector," declared Holmes, as brisk and breezy as I ever heard him. "Your suspect is one Henri or Louis Boulanger, formerly of Puerto de la Luz, Grand Canary, a citizen of France, who is to be arrested for the murder of Jules Boulanger, a lawful resident here for several years in the Wapping coal docks, and entitled to the protection of our law. Jules was probably killed by a blow from a heavy coal shovel you will readily find. He was one of the murderer's two elder brothers. The particular motive for the crime was to extinguish the claim of Jules Boulanger to share in the ownership of a family property in France --part of a valuable island in the River Seine. It is at Rouen, which serves as the seaport for Paris. I have already shared with you the details of the affairs of the Boulanger family at Rouen, and I can now tell you that the particular motive I mention may be much more serious in the law of France -- taken as part of a conspiracy to murder in course of breach of the Napoleonic Code protecting the democratic inheritance of property.

"A further assistance for you --and then a caution:

"The man you seek to arrest may have his head hidden in scarves or bandages, to hide white hair [unless he is shaven-headed, as many men go about in the coal trade]. He will almost certainly wear dark glasses to screen his eyes. That is because he is a victim of the physical variation known as albinism --a so-called albino-- whose body lacks the ability to make those pigments which colour our skin and hair and, most startlingly, the eyes. The eyes are left looking pink and transparent and --to some ignorant and superstitious people-- frightening and somehow evil. The suspect is one of two such younger exceptions in the Boulanger family --the other being his twin. That one has also been killed, though perhaps not murdered. These twins were driven out of Rouen by public prejudice, but they were provided with a fitful living working a small dockside depot in the Canary Islands bought by an elder brother --Marcel Boulanger, who sold out to the Hobson business on Madeira, as you know. I have learned that the Boulanger twins did not do well at Puerto de la Luz, despite being given free new lighters. There are very strong British companies in that port. An informant in Leadenhall Street tells me that Elder Dempster is behind 'the Grand Canary Coaling Company'

--formidable competition. There may well also have been the ancient prejudice at work there, against albinism. The backed-up losses, however caused, must have been carried for years by Marcel Boulanger. That explains his insistence that Mr Hobson take both island properties in their bargain, and it also explains why one twin should have sailed to Madeira, perhaps in search of recompense from his elder brother --or revenge. However, it is not now essential --"

Holmes stopped short, nodding across the inn yard to the tail end of the range of baskets on the quayside where three men with a coster's handcart had stopped to add four baskets to the line, roped in two pairs. Even at our distance we could see that one man was muffled up, if no more than someone might be who had a severe head cold. What could pass for a precaution for health's sake was made to look sinister, however, by a heavy mask, highwayman style, with eyeholes covered by dark glasses.

Morton started up, all his careful reservations abandoned at the sight of quarry, but Homes put out a restraining hand: "A few minutes, please, Morton. Let us give the goat time to pay the sheep, Hm? A least one other than the villain we see must be aware that there is more to those baskets than meets the eye."

Down on the roadside, the party at the wagon had easily taken down one pair of baskets, and set about lowering the second pair

--ironically rather gently, I thought-- nesting it to make a stack of four. Holmes continued to talk without taking his eyes off the doings on the street:

"Watson and I will be able to show you where those four baskets were hidden, Morton. That will help you win a confession, quite apart from the prime suspect's likely preference for being hanged rather than having his head chopped off. The carters there also have good reason to talk, since apparently they have helped to hide a capital crime."

Morton was visibly relieved, however, when the wagon driver pulled a heavy wedge from his footboard and kicked it under a front wheel before the trio strolled toward the inn, even contriving a thin smile limited to the corners of his mouth as Holmes got to his feet with a thin joke:

"At worst you'll be able to hold the lot of them for leaving a horse and cart unattended on a public thoroughfare. Save a fuss." Let us go down and see the wages of sin dispensed with refreshments. I wonder, Watson, how many crimes must have been paid for at the bar in this inn." Leaving me to cringe at this sally, Holmes turned to Morton:

"My caution, Inspector, Morton, has to do with the leanings of Scotland Yard. With the information you will possess, it may be judged more convenient to send the villain to the French police and the guillotine, so saving the trouble and expense of a trial. The authorities in Paris at present will be cheerfully disposed, I suspect, to welcome the prospect of chopping off the head of anybody named Boulanger. And for exposing a plot against the citizen's property protection in the sacred Republican law, they may find a medal for you. It will suit their present political stew."

With this, Holmes led the way down the open staircase to the long bar, mounted on ancient beer barrels on the ground floor. Emerging as we did from our position of vantage we were able to enter the taproom from a position chosen in advance, moving to it without apparent reference to any others present. The flow of business was out through the back of the building, lending only distant shouting and general hullabaloo to echo in the interior. We could hear nothing of what passed between our suspects but see well enough when accustomed to the gloom. Morton remained passive, perfectly restrained, until paper packets were passed to the carters. He spoke quietly then, but not to be contradicted:

"I must have those packets before they are opened, Holmes." And then, loudly: "Perhaps you will be good enough to go to the front door and look out for a cab."

"Of course, delighted!" Holmes responded in the same fashion, commanding attention and stumping off as suggested. Heads were raised to follow his progress, so that before they knew it Morton [not a very big man] stood over the seated trio to deliver his caution in ringing tones:

"I am Inspector Morton of Scotland Yard. You three men are under arrest for the offence of leaving a horse-drawn cart unattended on a public street, to the general danger. I will write down anything you say and it may be used in evidence."

The carter and his mate sat as if stunned by the consequence of this heinous crime they probably committed two or three times a day in an ordinary week's work. The muffled one, revealed as their employer, saw the front door blocked, flung back his stool and ran straight at me, well inside the yard door. Morton came to 'put the bracelets on him,' still sitting on the sawdust, but only after relieving the carters of the money they had been paid, opening the wrappings and swiftly counting it out under their noses.

"A wretched eleven pounds between them, Holmes," he complained later, "including the services of the horse. That may be just little enough to save them from a long stretch in Pentonville, or worse, for knowingly helping to conceal a capital crime. I think those two are not accomplices, but all three arrests are justifiable, considering what has to be in that basket on the wharf. My sergeant and a constable caught up with me while we were up on the balcony. They sat in the back yard over two glasses of ale they couldn't touch, but Sergeant Miller is an improver, Holmes. He boarded the ship and made inquiries --all above board, and interesting: she leaves half her load here and goes on to deliver the rest in Rouen. Is that merely a coincidence do you think? I'd rather keep the stack as it is, just for the present if you won't mind --not seeing the corpse, I mean."

"Not necessary at all, Morton, thank you."

"I expect you'll be glad to get back to Baker Street then, but I'll take you up on your offer to show me where the basket in the case was hidden. While we look at that, the constable will find you a cab from the High Street."

~0~

I left Holmes to make good on his offer, while I bundled up his *impedimenta* and collected our bill from the landlord --who volunteered not a word about events at his house that day. I could readily have believed, had he vouchsafed it were so, that nothing had happened in any way out of the ordinary. Nor had Holmes much to say on our rattle back to a grateful supper of cold meats and Mrs Hudson's excellent gravel pie. There awaited him a heap of papers and telegrams. From which he handed over only one telegram. It read:

"More for purpose to your inquiry: Madame Boulanger, widow of Didier, died sleeping Rouen yesterday in watch of daughter Garance Boulanger, and Marcel Boulanger, eldest son, who has returned from overseas. To your note inheritances here depend to be settled by judicial rule for Region Le Manche, needing months. Thank you.--Latouche, Loyd's Agent, Le Havre and Rouen."

I was looking forward to spending the night in my own bed, content to leave unanswered questions for the following day, and that *after* picking up the threads of my round of patients, but I could not resist putting the question: "Inheritances, Holmes? Pray how does that matter?" Do you not believe that Jules Boulanger was the victim of a plot by the albino twins to take over their elder brothers' coal yards? "

"There was indeed a plot, Watson, but more ambitious than you suggest. And it does have something to do with politics. It was rooted, one might almost say, in the French revolution. Morton is bound to be here for a chat tomorrow and perhaps we can discuss it then. Meanwhile, my compliments and thanks for her forbearance to your Mary. A great and fortunate case it was when you found her, Watson."

~0~

I was up and about at sparrows' breakfast on the morning after our return from Wapping Wall, and completed my morning round as soon as I could --reduced by two patients for whom my locum had signed death certificates. Locums never produce new patients to replace losses! I was still in good time for a brief interlude with

Holmes before Inspector Morton came almost noiselessly up the stairs after being announced by Mrs Hudson's Buttons. He was businesslike:

"It was the body of Mr Jules Boulanger in the basket, as you thought it would be, Mister Holmes, and he had been in it for some days. We can't say exactly because the villain, who is Henri Boulanger, can't remember, or says he can't. He is a genuine pink eye the police surgeon says, and it seems there are doctors to be found who say that such unfortunate people may not think in the way the rest of us do --partly because they are often persecuted --as happened in this case. The carter's men were using their employer's coal cart without his knowing and they knew there was a body in the basket. But they say --and the murderer confirms-- that he told them there was no money for a coffin and arrangements to return the body to France for burial. They are ignorant men and if there's no contrary evidence, that and the little money they were paid, will keep them out of prison. I don't feel any urge to put them away.

"It remains for me to thank you for your confidence in this case; it's a success we badly needed at the Yard right now. My thanks to you too, Doctor Watson --it's also a pleasure to work with you.

"And now, if you gentlemen will excuse me, I'll be on my way. I shall be all this day on the papers of the case, even though I have the confession."

"Oh, hang the confession, Holmes," I burst out after Morton drew the door shut behind him and went quietly down the stairs. How could you know. . ."

"A pipe, Watson? If it's not too early. And a brisk leg-stretcher in the Regent's park; there'll be a pretty frost around the lake and we'll get Wapping blown out out of our chests."

We strode along briskly enough with no lingering at the pretty lake, a happy relief for other strollers and hardy duck feeders; forgotten its mass drowning when two hundred citizens crashed through winter ice. At the Regent's Canal Holmes stopped, knocked out dottle on a heel, and refilled his pipe from the old slipper he had picked up and tucked inside his cape. From the shrubs that tempered the wind for us, the sluggish waterway affords direct passage to the London Docks. Looking down at the towpath, the matter of murder came up with Holmes as naturally as others might have been moved by the pretty waterscape:

"There must have been a plot between those twin younger brothers, Watson. This is one of those cases in which we must derive the motive from the circumstances: If a man is found drowned upside down in a butt of Madeira, it is reasonable to believe that he was up-ended in it by the parties known to have been last with him, acting in concert: so with the aggrieved Henri and Louis Boulanger, against their elder brothers, Marcel and Jules. The younger men must have been embittered at being driven out of France by an ancient prejudice. They did not do well in trade, and suffered a further blow when Marcel sold off his yards to Hobson, leaving them without income. They, with their mother and sister, were guaranteed equal shares in any property left by their father. This is the law of inheritance in France, under a revolutionary rule --now in the Napoleonic Code-- designed to break the custom that estates went to first sons, a practice that literally perpetuated the hold of powerful aristocrats, on the land of France. Looking for motive, I found that no legitimate French child may now be disinherited. That simple rule applied, of course, to the albino brothers. In looking for motive, I found the snag for the twins. The family property is on an island in the River Seine, and it is valuable. But all of it belongs to all the children. It cannot be divided or turned into gold unless all agree. I am told that properties in France go to ruin at times because of this rule, which extends indefinitely through the children of children . . . The younger brothers resolved, therefore, to kill the elder pair, leaving only a maiden lady to bend to their will. It makes little difference to the case for Morton, with a confession in hand and a simple case for revenge to bolster it.

"It seems inescapable, but does not matter critically in the outcome, any more than the superficially attractive and alarming suggestion that the younger Boulanger brothers, driven out of France by prejudice as soon as they were of age, were moved to violent reaction by the present face of French politics. There can be few market streets in France which do not exhibit the name of the general presently stirring up trouble, and there is a famous historical connection in France between violence and bread, or the lack of it. For a name, Boulanger is probably safer in France than anywhere else.

"In the case as it came to me, remarkably quickly and unusually as it did, there was confusion from the beginning. There was a vicious affair in the coalyard office, Watson, but the victor was the elder brother, Marcel. He delivered the fatal coup with the coal hammer but then brutally defaced the victim with the furnace rake --for one reason: he wanted to disguise the younger man's albinism, and use the device of muffling his own head and hiding his eyes as a disguise, to cover his escape, aboard *The Prospect of Whitby* --aided by the island's hurried funeral customs and his shocking mutilation of the corpse. Any hue and cry in Madeira would be set up after the wrong man.

"Confusion was there again when Marcel apparently 'skipped off safe into France' [as Morton complained] because Marcel had himself put ashore by boat at Honfleur, where there would be no official record. My supposition was that he could have gone up-river to Rouen but just as easily, immediately or later, have crossed or gone down-river into the port of Le Havre, to cross the Channel in the ferry to Southampton. My preference was for 'immediately.' There was no gain to be had from delay. There was a clue of sorts in the information given by the fugitive as copied from the ship's log. The French police must have laughed at the Yard when they were asked to look for "Roger Dileel of Marseilles," wanted for murder. Even the simplest-minded gendarme would have recognized the misleading play on the name of Rouget de L'Isle, author of *La Marseillaise*!

"So we were late, Watson, in shifting to the Wapping Wall tavern. Marcel Boulanger got there before us. That is my reasoning from the elaborately decorated shirt, a rare example of Madeiran peasant work, I'd guess, purely on the honest-enough word of the washerwoman who was certain that it was too fine to be French. Our leading suspect had time to depart in an orderly way, paying his bill --so sealing the innkeeper's lips, but not, fortunately for us, the potman's. It is my belief that the disguised Marcel, from the vantage point of the Prospect probably spotted the remaining younger Boulanger in similar cover, and decided there and then to drop the simple disguise and return to France. it must have seemed to him that there was virtually no chance of the Madeira murder being brought home to him. If it ever were he could with impunity plead self-defence. But by leaving Jules and the other young brother to each other, there was every chance of reducing the brotherhood of the Boulangers to one: himself: one more being murdered and a third [with a little assistance, perhaps] executed. That, Watson, is what I think has happened. Now it is necessary to boil all this down into a telegram, wherewith to submit my account. It's a pretty penny for the result, Watson, though Mr Hobson of Funchal will have the satisfaction of knowing that one of the pair who murdered his son in Grand Canary is actually buried in the English cemetery in Madeira, and the other is likely soon to be hanged in London."

"And Mr Hobson must be content with that, I suppose," I offered, uncomfortably. "But Marcel Boulanger is set up in Rouen, beneficiary of two killings; one he committed [perhaps in self defence, as you say] but the other resulting from his abandoning Wapping knowing that he was leaving the space clear for one of his remaining brothers to kill the other. It is really quite shameful, Holmes. Is nothing to be done?"

"You are right, Watson, but that is not a result I intend to leave undisputed. Once Morton has had his moment of glory I shall be sending the Chief of Police of La Manche, at Rouen --with explanations-- the gift of a beautifully embroidered shirt, recovered from Wapping and known to have been worn there by Marcel Boulanger, lately returned to the family property in France. To become the owner of that inheritance he will have to show that his three brothers are dead. One is buried in Madeira, but under Marcel's own identity; another, Henri, is in police hands in London, accused of murdering the third, Jules --found dead in a coal basket [probably as a result of being brained with a shovel] when the basket was about to be shipped to France. This despite the usual conveniences of a Wapping Wall murder, interment in a derelict yard or, safer still, the Thames. Why Henri dangerously held back his disposal of the body to stow it into *The Prospect of Whitby* will probably always be a subject for speculation unless it emerges from the trial. I am inclined to think that it was to cause a sensation in France, where a magistrate must consider everything that is known about a case of confused inheritance. It may be many years, Watson, before one can be found to put the stamp of official approval on any inheritance by Marcel Boulanger of Rouen."

~o~0~o~

WHAT EARLY READERS HAD TO SAY

Here are some Amazonian notices for OLIVER ST GAUDY's first two Dvanda Masda Books-in-Brief series of Sherlock Holmes memoirs:

The series of Oliver's modest offerings began quietly with <u>The Case of the Lost Lion of Lithuania</u>, written as the mystery it remains, probably never to be elucidated since it closed with an unseen shipwreck. It gained one five-star review and a couple of two-star sniffs, one carping at the care taken to convey unusual features of locations substantially unchanged to this day.

A quite justifiable complaint with general application arose because a footnote was distractingly misplaced: not obviously easy to avoid in an e-book. It will be moved to the end of the text in a new edition. The same plan is adopted in the latest case history.

Delphine C. Moyer rated the case "a great book."

~0~

<u>The Case of the West London Wives</u>, a story of blackmail, with similar attention to locations relatively unchanged today but a different class of cast, quickly netted five five-star notices and one four-star: 86 per cent of the reviews.

Delphine, economical with words welcomed another "great book."

Drstatz recorded: Exceptionally well done. This is closer to a short story than a novella. Regardless, it is a masterful outing. The plot is tight and the reader's interest is kept throughout. Settings, characterizations and other elements are done to perfection with enough twists and turns to satisfy the most demanding reader. In short, this is a perfect story for when you want to settle in and enjoy a taut, well-presented adventure. I look forward to more of Mr St Gaudy's works.

John E: "A different side of Homes who sees clues and problems in a different perspective. I liked the way the story unfolded.

borky chutzpah: Thank you, Oliver St. Gaudy. Having read many Holmes Pastiches I've occasionally been tempted to write a review of some very good ones as well as some at the other end of the spectrum. I have recently read some very bad ones but I believe I would have written my very positive reaction to Mr. Gaudy's excellent effort even without my recent disappointments with other pastiches. Holmes and Watson are depicted as capable gentlemen --Holmes naturally much more so-- and their relationship not predicated upon Holmes belittling Watson and throwing melodramatic hissy fits. There is incisive intelligence, mutual respect and, of course, Holmes' brilliant insights and handling of the dilemma presented to him. The style is very Conan Doyle, perhaps even more like the Solar Pons stories which I greatly enjoy. Don't be fooled by the cartoonish cover - this is top notch stuff. I enjoyed this more than Mr. Gaudy's other book --the Lion of Lithuania-- which is still superior to many other pastiches. I hope Mr. Gaudy receives the accolades and appreciative readership he richly deserves.

hiram: Good read. The only bad thing it is too short!!! Holmes shows again how logic and observation can and do often solve crimes, in books and in real life. This is a good read, and confirms my opinion of Sherlock novels.

Amazon Customer: Short but sweet. Totally plausible and fun Holmes book. Short enough to get through quickly but long enough for details. His old English is fun.

Four Star Review pictured the book as "forgery with a twist."

38174291R00041

Made in the USA
Charleston, SC
30 January 2015